Written by Gaby Goldsack
Illustrated by Steve Smallman

This edition published by Parragon in 2010

Parragon
Queen Street House
4 Queen Street
Bath BA1 1HE, UK

ISBN 978-1-4454-1104-0

Printed in China

The Tricky Tractor

Parragon

Bath · New York · Singapore · Hong Kong · Cologne · Delhi · Melbourne

One sunny morning, Farmer Fred's wife, Jenny, shooed him from the kitchen.

"I don't want any muddy boots on my sparkly clean floor," said Jenny.

Farmer Fred looked around the farmyard. There was junk everywhere, the paint was peeling from the henhouse, the gates were squeaking and the muck-heap had spread all over the farmyard.

"This farmyard could do with a good clean too," he decided.

"Woof! Woof!" barked Patch the sheepdog.

Farmer Fred decided to paint the hen-house first. He balanced his pot of paint on the tractor bonnet. Then he set to work with his paintbrush.

"Woof!" barked Patch as Farmer Fred dripped paint over the tractor's dusty bonnet.

"You're right, Patch!" said Farmer Fred. "The hen-house looks as good as new." Hetty Hen clucked in agreement.

"But these paint splashes will be tricky to get off the tractor," grumbled Farmer Fred.

"Now let's sort out those squeaky gates," said Farmer Fred. "All they need is a bit of oil."

But as Farmer Fred jumped into the tractor, the bonnet gave a noisy creak and sprang open.

"Dithering doorknobs!" complained Farmer Fred. "This bonnet is getting tricky to close." He tied it up with string and drove around the farm oiling the creaky gates, singing as he went.

"Hi-ho, hi-ho! It's off to work I go, with a tractor and a dog, all day I slog! Hi-ho, hi-ho!"

As Farmer Fred drove past the barn his nose began to twitch.

"It's about time we got rid of that smelly muck-heap, Patch!" he said.

He loaded the muck-spreader with dung and hitched it to the tractor. The tractor towed it across the fields spreading the dung over the ground. Before long, the tractor's windscreen was covered in flyaway dung.

"Walloping cowpats! This windscreen is so dirty, it's tricky seeing where I'm going," grumbled Farmer Fred.

"Woof!" agreed Patch.

When they got back to the farmyard Farmer Fred looked at all the junk lying around.

"Let's take this lot to the dump, Patch," said Farmer Fred. He hitched the trailer to the tractor and loaded up the junk.

But as he drove through the farm gate, Farmer Fred didn't notice a rusty old rake on the ground. The tractor drove straight over it.

Hissss! One of its huge tyres had a puncture. The tractor bumped along the road.

"This tractor is getting really tricky to drive," grumbled Farmer Fred.

When Farmer Fred got back to the farmyard, he felt very pleased with himself.

"Everything is neat and tidy," he smiled. But then he noticed the tractor. "That old tractor is past its best," he said. "It looks like the scrapyard for you."

Farmer Fred jumped into the tractor and turned the key.

Nothing happened. He jumped out of the tractor and untied the bonnet.

"Hmm, this is going to be tricky," he thought, scratching his head. "How am I going to get this old tractor to the scrapyard now?"

"Never fear, I've an idea!" Farmer Fred said suddenly.

As Farmer Fred disappeared into his workshop, the animals gathered round.

"Poor old tractor," sighed Harry Horse. "All it needs is some..."

But before Harry Horse had finished, Farmer Fred came out of the workshop.

"This," said Farmer Fred, "is my Lift-and-tow Crane. Just the thing for towing tractors."

Farmer Fred attached the Lift-and-tow Crane to the back of his pick-up truck, and started cranking the back of the tractor off the ground.

Farmer Fred jumped into the pick-up truck and started the engine.

"I'll tow this old tractor out of here before you can say **Brussels sprouts!**" he shouted, revving his engine.

But before he had moved an inch, there was a loud CRUNCH! as the Lift-and-tow Crane crumpled and the tractor crashed to the ground.

"Woof!" cried Patch.

"Cluck!" cried Hetty Hen.

"Oink!" cried Polly Pig.

"Tearaway turnips," yelled Farmer Fred. "How am I going to shift this old tractor now?"

Crunch!

Farmer Fred sat down to think. He didn't know what he was going to do with such a tricky tractor.

The animals gathered around the poor old tractor.

"The tractor's been so busy, it's probably run out of petrol," said Harry Horse.

"It needs a wash," said Connie Cow.

"And a lick of paint," said Polly Pig.

"A drop of oil would fix the bonnet," said Shirley Sheep.

"Don't forget the tyre," said Hetty Hen.

"We'll have to tell Farmer Fred," said Patch.

While Farmer Fred sat thinking, the
animals got to work. Shirley Sheep
knocked over the petrol can. Polly Pig
tipped the oil-can out of the tractor.
Harry Horse kicked over the water barrel.

"Hey, stop making a mess in my nice clean farmyard!" cried Farmer Fred, as Patch brought over the paintbrush. But then he smiled. "I've got a brilliant idea – I'll spring-clean the tractor!"

Farmer Fred got to work straight away.

First of all, he gave the tractor a good wash.

Then he oiled the bonnet and fixed the puncture.

Then he gave it a fresh coat of bright red paint.

Last of all, he filled it up with petrol.

As Farmer Fred and the animals stood back to admire his handiwork, Jenny came out of the farmhouse.

"That tractor looks as good as new," said Jenny.

"As I've always said," smiled Farmer Fred, "there are years left in my trusty tractor yet." Jenny looked at Patch and smiled.